Animal Word Puzzles
Coloring Book

Nina Barbaresi

Dover Publications, Inc.
New York

Note

This book is a collection of eight different kinds of puzzles—84 puzzles in all. These puzzles will show you how much fun you can have with reading and spelling—especially when the subject is animals! The pictures in this book have been drawn so that you can also have a lot of fun coloring them in!

Published in Canada by General Publishing Company, Ltd., 30 Lesmill Road, Don Mills, Toronto, Ontario.
Published in the United Kingdom by Constable and Company, Ltd., 3 The Lanchesters, 162–164 Fulham Palace Road, London W6 9ER.

Animal Word Puzzles Coloring Book is a new work, first published by Dover Publications, Inc., in 1991.

International Standard Book Number: 0-486-26848-9

Manufactured in the United States of America
Dover Publications, Inc., 31 East 2nd Street, Mineola, N.Y. 11501

Search-a-Word Puzzles (pages 1–6)

The names of all the things pictured are hidden in the puzzles. We've already found the word FISH for you. Can you find the others?

B	S	P	Y	N	A
D	O	G	W	J	V
E	L	Z	T	C	F
Q	F	J	P	A	W
O	I	V	R	T	D
R	S	L	E	K	S
I	H	B	A	X	T
U	F	E	Y	E	Z

C	K	S	Z	L	T
A	M	Y	E	X	C
M	A	J	L	T	M
E	W	B	K	R	O
L	D	P	V	Q	L
E	U	N	O	S	E
P	F	T	G	N	I
L	E	G	O	H	S

E	L	O	I	U	P
Z	T	K	C	E	A
B	A	B	O	O	N
E	P	L	B	C	T
H	I	A	R	O	H
O	R	C	A	M	E
D	N	I	E	P	R
P	U	F	F	I	N

P	A	R	R	O	T
E	U	T	F	V	N
L	C	B	K	H	A
X	R	W	Z	O	I
B	A	T	N	O	K
P	B	D	Y	F	H
C	S	M	G	R	O
J	I	B	E	E	Q

I	F	O	O	T	Q
M	J	S	V	H	W
O	B	R	S	P	A
U	L	O	E	X	P
S	C	Y	A	K	Y
E	N	U	L	D	J
G	F	M	E	T	K
H	O	R	N	Z	F

H	S	N	A	I	L
B	I	T	L	U	J
G	C	H	I	C	K
A	K	F	O	Q	E
N	G	Y	N	V	C
R	Z	L	X	M	L
T	U	S	K	W	A
O	P	C	D	N	W

Fill-in-the-Blanks Puzzles (pages 7–11)

Can you spell the names of these things? We've made it easier for you by supplying some of the letters already.

P _ _ _ R B _ _ R

H _ _ M _ _ G B _ _ D

S _ _ _ F _ S _

M _ S Q _ _ T _

G _ _ _ S H _ _ P _ R

S _ _ H _ R _ E

W _ O D _ H _ _ K

SC _ _ P _ _ N

J _ _ K R _ _ B _ T

P _ _ G _ _ N

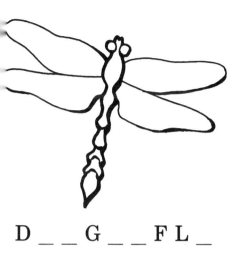

D _ _ G _ _ F L _

O _ T _ _ _ S

S _ L _ _ _ N D _ _

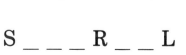

S _ _ _ R _ _ L

K _ _ G _ R _ O

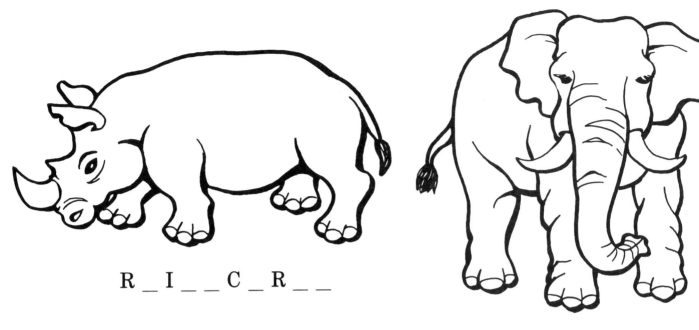

R _ I _ _ C _ R _ _

E _ _ P _ _ N _

C _ O _ _ D _ L _

G _ _ _ F _ E

G _ _ IL _ A

R _ _ N _ _ E _

R _ _ D _ _ N _ E _

B _ _ T _ R F _ _

C _ Y _ _ E

H _ _ P _ _ _ T _ M _ S

Crossword Puzzles (pages 12–23)

Print the names of the pictured things in the appropriate squares of the puzzles. We've already done 1 Across and 1 Down for you.

1.

Across

Down

1.

3.

2.

5.

4.

1.

2.

3.

3.

4.

5.

2.

1.

3.

2.

4.

5.

Across   Down

1.   1.

3.   2.

4.   4.

Across

Down

1.

1.

2.

2.

3.

4.

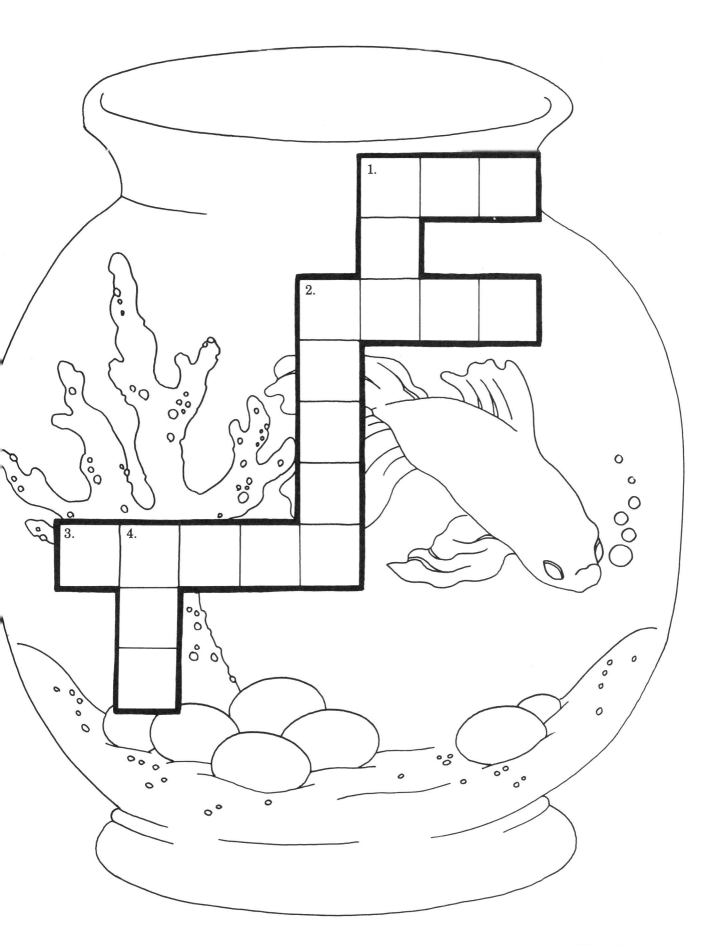

Across

Down

1.

1.

2.

3.

4.

4.

On each of these pages there are *three* animals that begin with the pictured letter. Can you find them?

S

D

P

Scrambled Word Puzzles (pages 28–30)

Can you put the letters in the right order to spell out the names of the animals pictured?

UYKERT

RAHSK

ESORTOR

EOML

ORDAPLE

IORNB

OXF

BLAM

RINCADAL

UKDC

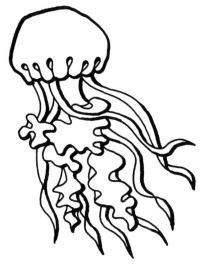

YELJHILSF

LUGL

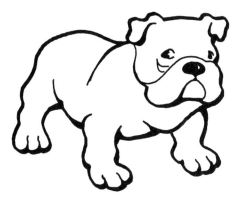

LUDBOLG

RTOAPR

NEKSA

Number Code Puzzles (pages 31–34)

Spell the names of these animals by referring to the code at the top of each page, which tells you which letter to use for each number. We've done the first puzzle for you.

A	B	C	D	E	F	G	H	I	J	K	L	M	N	O	P	Q	R	S	T	U	V	W	X	Y	Z
1	2	3	4	5	6	7	8	9	10	11	12	13	14	15	16	17	18	19	20	21	22	23	24	25	26

10	1	25
J	A	Y

13	15	20	8

18	1	2	2	9	20

5	12	11

15	23	12

A	B	C	D	E	F	G	H	I	J	K	L	M	N	O	P	Q	R	S	T	U	V	W	X	Y	Z
1	2	3	4	5	6	7	8	9	10	11	12	13	14	15	16	17	18	19	20	21	22	23	24	25	26

19	5	1	12

8	1	23	11

3	12	1	13

8	5	14

26	5	2	18	1

A	B	C	D	E	F	G	H	I	J	K	L	M	N	O	P	Q	R	S	T	U	V	W	X	Y	Z
1	2	3	4	5	6	7	8	9	10	11	12	13	14	15	16	17	18	19	20	21	22	23	24	25	26

12	5	13	13	9	14	7

9	13	16	1	12	1

19	1	14	4	16	9	16	5	18

3	15	12	12	9	5

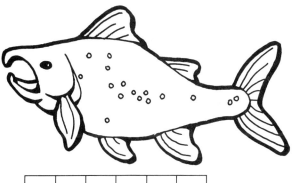

19	1	12	13	15	14

A	B	C	D	E	F	G	H	I	J	K	L	M	N	O	P	Q	R	S	T	U	V	W	X	Y	Z
1	2	3	4	5	6	7	8	9	10	11	12	13	14	15	16	17	18	19	20	21	22	23	24	25	26

15	20	20	5	18

18	1	20

3	8	9	3	11

23	1	19	16

8	15	18	19	5

Draw a line to connect each animal with its name.

MUSKRAT

WALRUS

MOTH

CUB

FAWN

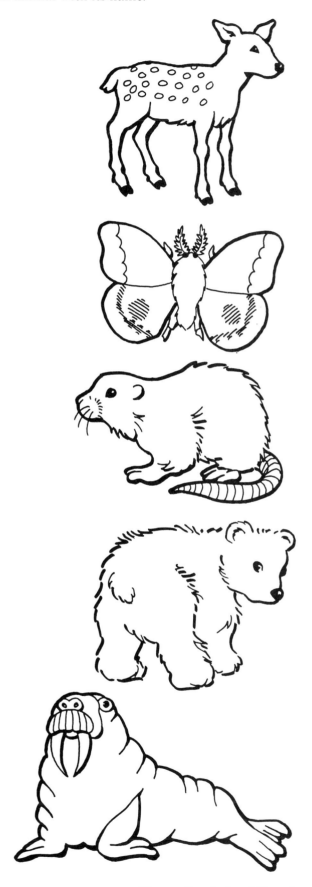

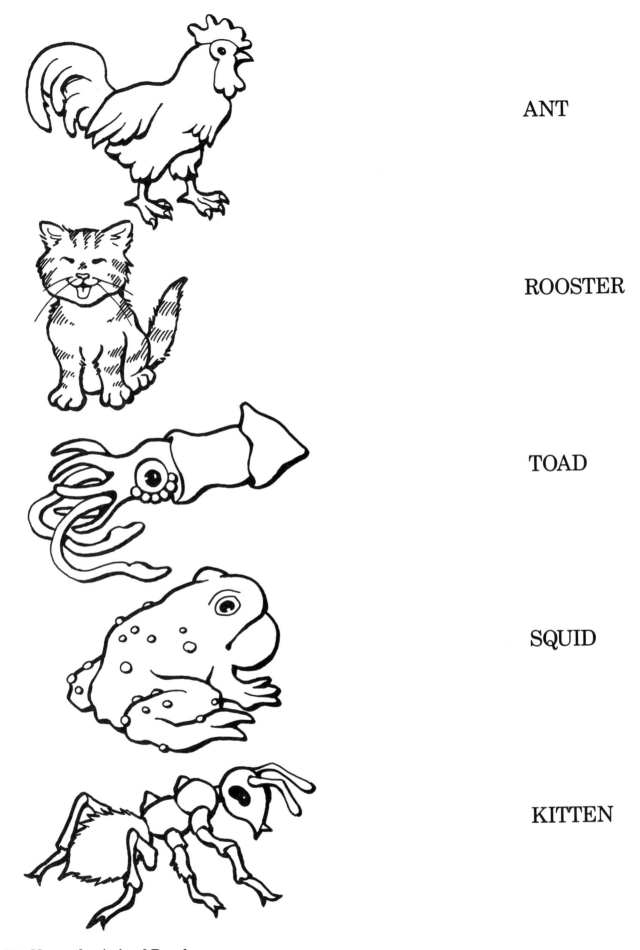

ANT

ROOSTER

TOAD

SQUID

KITTEN

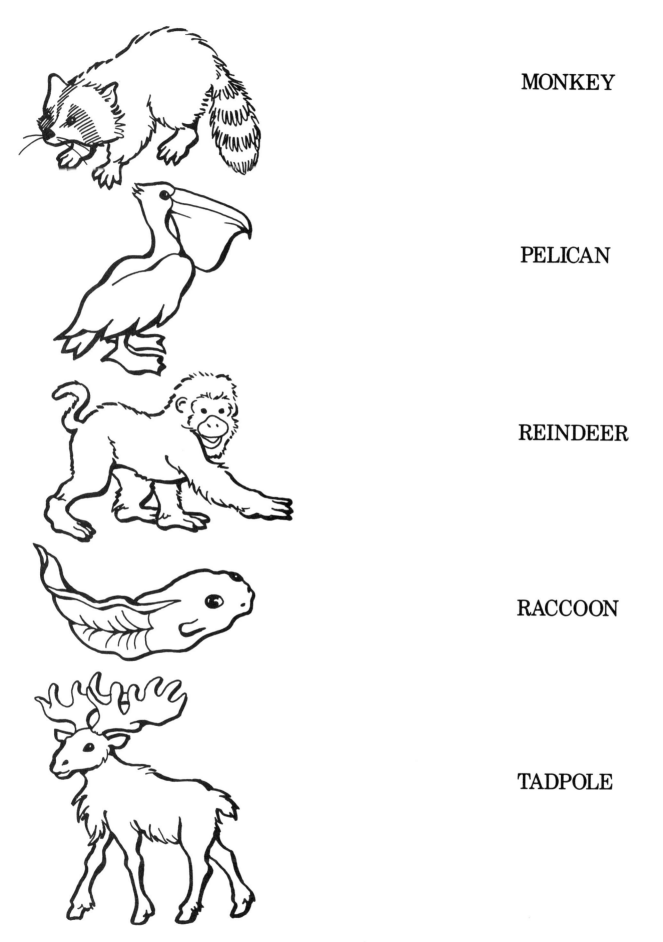

MONKEY

PELICAN

REINDEER

RACCOON

TADPOLE

Hidden Names Puzzle (page 38)

Can you find each animal's name hidden in the sentence underneath the picture? We've done the first one for you.

He'd like to be a redhead.

Please don't sell a mad dog.

Margo ate the whole pie.

Eli only has three cents.

Visit Africa, Melanie!

Solutions

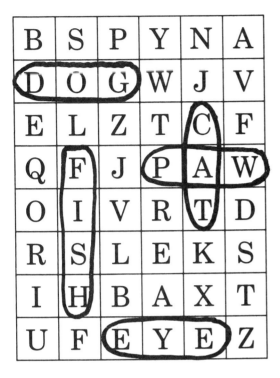

page 1

page 2

page 3

page 4

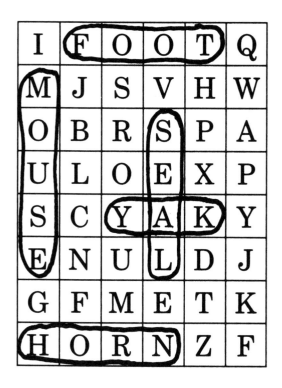

page 5

H	S	N	A	I	L
B	I	T	L	U	J
G	C	H	I	C	K
A	K	F	O	Q	E
N	G	Y	N	V	C
R	Z	L	X	M	L
T	U	S	K	W	A
O	P	C	D	N	W

page 6

P _ _ _ R   B _ _ R

POLAR BEAR

H _ _ M _ _ GB _ _ D

HUMMINGBIRD

S _ _ H _ R _ E

SEAHORSE

W _ OD _ H _ _ K

WOODCHUCK

S _ _ _ F _ S _

STARFISH

SC _ _ P _ _ N

SCORPION

M _ SQ _ _ T _

MOSQUITO

G _ _ _ SH _ _ P _ R

GRASSHOPPER

J _ _ KR _ _ B _ T

JACKRABBIT

P _ _ G _ _ N

PENGUIN

page 7

page 8

D _ _ G _ _ FL _

DRAGONFLY

O _ T _ _ _ S

OCTOPUS

R _ I _ _ C _ R _ _

RHINOCEROS

E _ _ P _ _ N _

ELEPHANT

S _ L _ _ _ ND _ _

SALAMANDER

C _ O _ _ D _ L _

CROCODILE

S _ _ _ R _ _ L

SQUIRREL

K _ _ G _ R _ O

KANGAROO

G _ _ _ F _ E

GIRAFFE

G _ _ IL _ A

GORILLA

page 9

page 10

R _ _ N _ _ E _

REINDEER

R _ _ D _ _ N _ E _

ROADRUNNER

B _ _ T _ RF _ _

BUTTERFLY

C _ Y _ _ E

COYOTE

H _ _ P _ _ _ T _ M _ S

HIPPOPOTAMUS

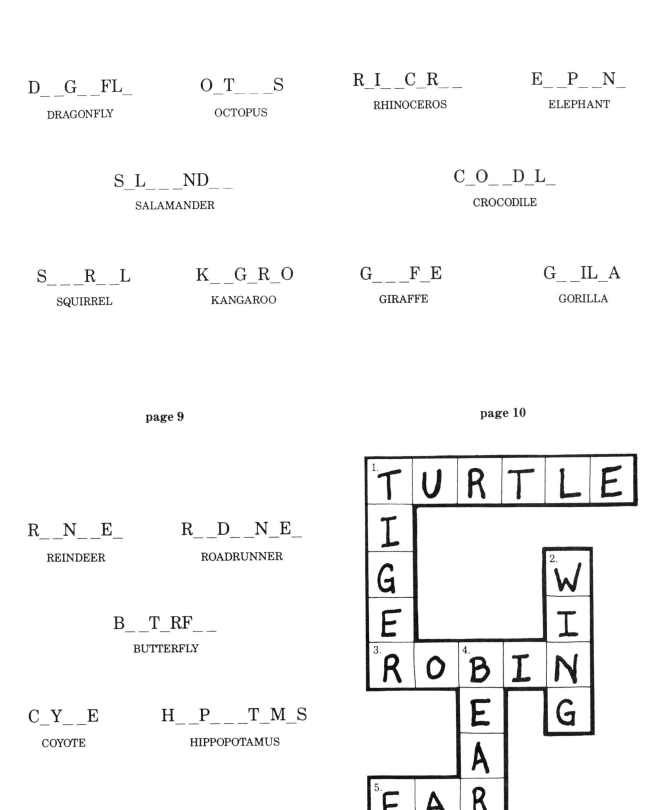

page 11

page 13

page 15

page 17

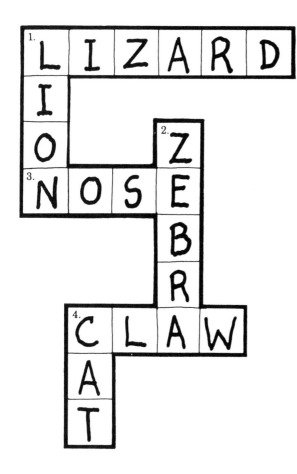

page 19

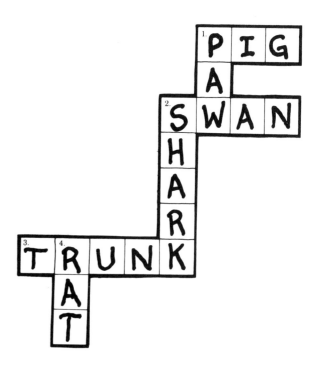

page 21

page 23

page 24

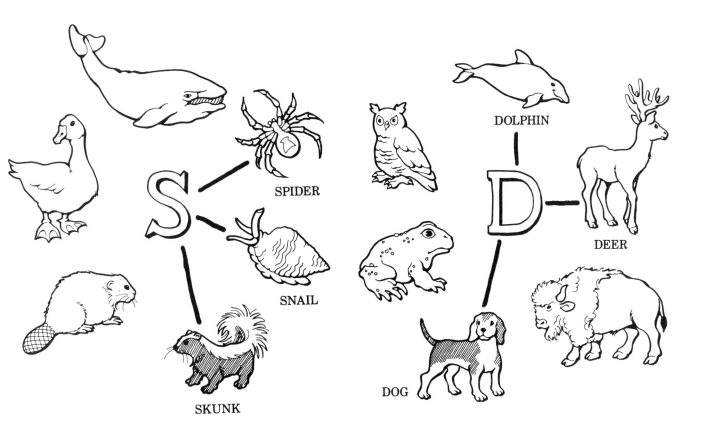

page 25

page 26

PORCUPINE

PENGUIN

PANDA

UYKERT
TURKEY

RAHSK
SHARK

ESORTOR
ROOSTER

EOML
MOLE

ORDAPLE
LEOPARD

page 27

page 28

IORNB
ROBIN

OXF
FOX

BLAM
LAMB

RINCADAL
CARDINAL

UKDC
DUCK

YELJHILSF
JELLYFISH

LUGL
GULL

LUDBOLG
BULLDOG

RTOAPR
PARROT

NEKSA
SNAKE

page 29

page 30

10	1	25
J	A	Y

13	15	20	8
M	O	T	H

19	5	1	12
S	E	A	L

8	1	23	11
H	A	W	K

18	1	2	2	9	20
R	A	B	B	I	T

3	11	1	13
C	L	A	M

5	12	11
E	L	K

15	23	12
O	W	L

8	5	14
H	E	N

26	5	2	18	1
Z	E	B	R	A

page 31

page 32

12	5	13	13	9	14	7
L	E	M	M	I	N	G

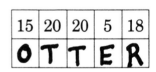

15	20	20	5	18
O	T	T	E	R

18	1	20
R	A	T

9	13	16	1	12	1
I	M	P	A	L	A

19	1	14	4	16	9	16	5	18
S	A	N	D	P	I	P	E	R

3	8	9	3	11
C	H	I	C	K

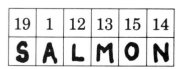

3	15	12	12	9	5
C	O	L	L	I	E

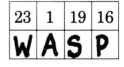

23	1	19	16
W	A	S	P

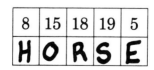

8	15	18	19	5
H	O	R	S	E

19	1	12	13	15	14
S	A	L	M	O	N

page 33

page 34

MUSKRAT

WALRUS

MOTH

CUB

FAWN

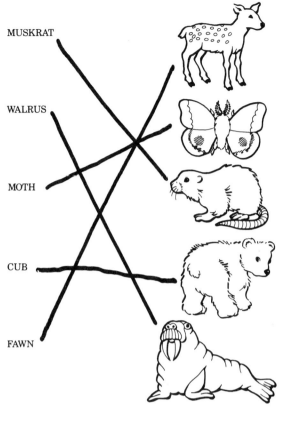

page 35

ANT

ROOSTER

TOAD

SQUID

KITTEN

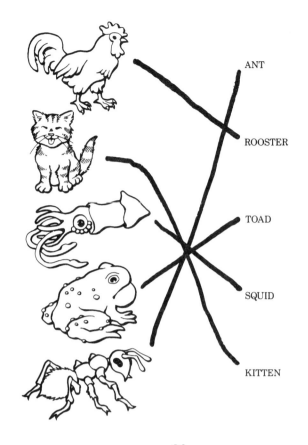

page 36

MONKEY

PELICAN

REINDEER

RACCOON

TADPOLE

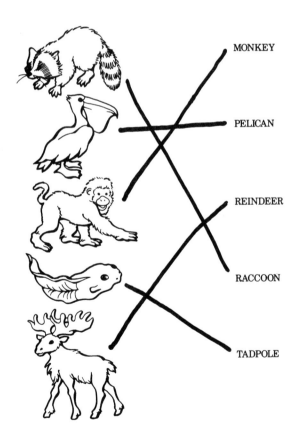

page 37

Please don't sell a mad dog.

He'd like to be a redhead.

Margo ate the whole pie.

Eli only has three cents.

Visit Africa, Melanie!

page 38